The Mockingbird Mystery

Marianne Hering

Chariot Victor Publishing
A Division of Cook Communications

Chariot Victor Publishing
A division of Cook Communications, Colorado Springs, Colorado 80918
Cook Communications, Paris, Ontario
Kingsway Communications, Eastbourne, England

THE MOCKINGBIRD MYSTERY
© 1998 by Marianne Hering

Edited by Kathy Davis
Designed by Andrea Boven
Cover illustration by Matthew Archambault

First printing, 1998
Printed in the United States of America
02 01   5 4 3 2

Library of Congress Cataloging-in-Publication Data

Hering, Marianne.
    The mockingbird mystery / Marianne Hering.
        p.   cm. – (White House adventures ; 2)
    Summary: While staying with their grandfather, President Thomas
Jefferson, at the White House, Ellen Randolph and her brother and sister
try to discover what is behind a series of strange occurrences, including a
broken skeleton, a picked lock, and information leaked to the newspapers.
    ISBN 0-7814-3065-8
    1. Jefferson, Thomas, 1743-1826–Juvenile fiction.   [1. Jefferson,
Thomas, 1743-1826–Fiction. 2. Grandfathers–Fiction. 3. Brothers and sisters–
Fiction. 4. Mystery and detective stories.]   I. Title. II. Series: Hering,
Marianne. White House adventures; 2.
PZ7.H431258Mo 1998
[Fic]–dc21   98-26432
                                                                CIP
                                                                AC

To my dear mother:
Mary Agnes Oakes Kendrick

CHAPTER

The Puzzle

Nine-year-old Ellen sat at her grandfather's table in the library of the President's House. She carefully cut the outline of a paper doll with a sharp pair of scissors. When she had finished, she held up a chain of eight little girls holding hands.

Ellen next began to work on a puzzle her grandfather had given her that morning. While she was thinking, she dipped her quill into black ink. Flowers appeared as she drew neatly around the edges of the poem.

> I've seen the sea all in a blaze of fire
> I've seen a house high as the moon and higher
> I've seen the sun at twelve o'clock at night
> I've seen the man who saw this wondrous sight

"Jeff," she asked her older brother, "can you figure this out? Grandpapa said everything in this poem is true, even if it doesn't seem so at first."

The youth grunted and ignored the paper Ellen held out to him across the large wooden table. He didn't even look away from the squirrel skeleton he was putting together.

The ribcage was in place, and Jeff was using tweezers to hold the tiny neck bones while he glued them on.

"Oh, let me look at the silly paper," Anne sighed. Ellen's sister put her own quill into a special holder. "It should be simple."

But after Anne read the poem, she wrinkled her nose. "This is nonsense," the fourteen-year-old girl said. "Whoever heard of water burning or the sun out at midnight?"

"That's it!" Ellen cried. "I think that's a clue. Isn't there an old story about the sun staying up for a whole day? I'm going to look for a Bible." When she stood, the light from the window fell on the ringlets of her light red hair. She took after her grandfather, President Thomas Jefferson, in many ways; her hair color being only one of them. Like him, she loved books, poetry, and thinking for herself.

Anne had soft brown hair and thought of only one thing: growing up. That morning she was writing a letter to her friend Emily Smithers about what it was like at the President's House. At a recent dinner party, John Quincy Adams had called her a lady. "Mr. Adams is not some country boy," Anne wrote. "He has lived in New England and in Europe. The senator knows about proper society. If he says I am a lady, then who is Mama to say I am not?"

Jeff, who was really named Thomas Jefferson Randolph after his grandfather, was no bookworm like Ellen. Nor did he want to grow up fast like Anne. He was a tall thirteen-year-old, husky for his age, and he loved the outdoors. He felt cramped inside the President's House and longed for his home in Virginia. In the country, he could ride on a horse all day or hike through the woods. But as long as he was in Washington City, Jeff had to stay inside most of the time. His mother was worried that if he went out too much, the stinky city air would make him ill.

While Ellen searched the many bookcases for a Bible, Anne went to the library window. Lined up on the windowsill sat a row of potted roses. Anne knew each variety by its proper name. She peeled off the dead petals from one pink rose that was just past blooming.

In a cage hanging near the window, the president kept a pet mockingbird. "Oooo, poor baby," said Anne softly to the gray-and-white bird. "You want to come out and play, I can tell."

She opened the cage and stuck in her finger. The bird hopped onto it. As she gently brought him out, the mockingbird twittered.

"He is so cute," Anne said to Jeff. "I'm glad that Mama gave him to Grandpapa. He loves to listen to him sing."

Jeff looked up from his brownish-white bones. "How do you know it's a he? They all look alike to me."

"Grandpapa named him Pegasus," said Anne. "That's a boy's name."

Ellen came out from behind a bookcase and frowned. "Anne, put him back. We're not supposed to disturb anything in Grandpapa's study. Do you want to have to stay upstairs in the nursery with Mama and the girls?"

"He may send *you* there," Anne said. "But I'm almost fifteen and a *lady*. Grandpapa gave me the key to the study. I may come and go anywhere I choose. I won't have to go to the nursery."

Anne was right. Ellen knew both Anne and Jeff were safe from having to stay with Mother if they got into trouble. But she was much younger. Nine wasn't too old to stay with her three younger sisters, Cornelia, age six, Virginia, age four, and Mary, age two.

Ellen didn't say anything else as Anne let the bird sit on her shoulder while she finished her letter. Ellen finally came back to the table with a book. "I found three New Testaments. One is in Greek, one in French, and one in English. But look at the English one. It's all torn up."

Both Anne and Jeff gasped when they saw the scraps of paper that had once been a thin leather-bound book. The three Randolph children knew that their grandfather loved books almost as much as he loved his grandchildren. From the very first time they ever sat on his warm lap to hear a story, he taught them how to hold a book. Their hands had to be clean before touching one. They knew not to crack the spine. Books were never to get dusty or wet. And above all, they were never to tear the pages.

Jeff took the book from his sister's small white hands. "It's not really torn," he said. "Someone cut this Bible neatly with a knife or sharp scissors, like the pair you used for the paper dolls. On almost every page, something is missing."

"Put the book back," said Anne. "I know I won't have to go to the nursery, but I couldn't bear it if Grandpapa thought we did it. He would be so cross. And he might not let us in here anymore. It would be horrid. Put it back."

"Put what back?" asked a familiar voice from the door-way. The three Randolph children turned around to see their grandfather leaning against the doorframe, his shoulders a bit stooped. He had on his usual worn clothes made from handspun material.

But something was missing: He wasn't wearing his usual, warm, comfortable smile.

CHAPTER

2

The Punishment

The three children all spoke at once. The noise of their shouts scared Pegasus, who flapped his clipped wings and fluttered from Anne's shoulder to the president's.

Anne's voice was the loudest, and she got her grandfather's attention first. "I never touched that book," she said. "I've been writing letters the whole time. It was Ellen."

Jeff was next. The tattered papers were still in his hands. "Ellen did bring me the book," he said. "This is the first I've seen of it." He put the book down on the table and pushed it toward Ellen. He looked at his younger sister, who was near to tears. "But I don't think she did it on purpose," Jeff added. "Ellen loves books as much as you do."

Ellen couldn't speak to defend herself. She wanted to throw herself into her grandfather's arms, but she was too big for that now. With Anne and Jeff telling the same story, it was two against one. A lump of fear stuck in her throat like mashed potatoes.

Her grandfather's face looked stern and gray as ash.

"Anne," the president asked in his quiet but firm voice,

"what do you think the punishment should be for cutting up a book?"

Anne felt grown-up because her grandfather was asking her advice. She paused before speaking to consider her words. When she answered, it was with all the dignity of a county judge. "Well," she said, "Ellen must make amends and pay for the damage. And I think you should ban her from the study until she's thirteen, like Jeff. And, she has to miss the New Year's Party. After all, it wasn't just any old book, but a *Bible*."

The president rubbed his chin and nodded as if he thought that was a good idea. He turned to Jeff next. "And what do you think should be the punishment for cutting up a book?"

Jeff looked at Ellen again. He didn't know what to say. He liked his younger sister and didn't want to see her get into trouble. He didn't think she really cut the book. But after all, there were the scissors she had been using. And she had been behind the bookcase a long while. She could have done it. . . . "The person who did it," he said, "should have tea alone in her room. She won't do it again."

Then their grandfather turned to Ellen. His eyes were narrowed and his lips in a scowl. She took a quick breath and stepped back from him, bumping into the table as she did so.

He asked in a gruff voice, "Ellen, which punishment do you think is fair?"

Ellen didn't think either was fair because she had not ruined the book. But it seemed her grandfather believed her brother and sister. Ellen didn't try to defend herself. There was nothing she could say. It was her word against Anne's and Jeff's. "I think missing the family tea is enough," Ellen said. Her voice was no louder than the whisper of butterfly wings.

"Well, then," answered Thomas Jefferson, "that is to be the punishment. . . . It looks as if I am to have tea in my bedroom. For you see, I cut the book."

*   *   *   *   *

Just before Ellen sat down at the family table to eat, a servant, one of the coffee-skinned slaves brought from the Randolph's home in Virginia, delivered a note to Ellen.

She unfolded the heavy parchment paper and read her grandfather's distinctive writing: "Please join me for tea in my bedchamber. It is too harsh a punishment to eat alone."

Ellen had never eaten a meal with just her grandfather before. At the family table in Virginia, her mother, father, four sisters, cousins, and brother were there. And she wasn't old enough to attend the small dinner parties her grandfather gave at the President's House or at his Virginia home. This was a rare moment for her. She raced to his room, passing her very pregnant mother on the wide main staircase. Mrs. Randolph, who waddled with each step down, warned, "Slow yourself, Ellen. Your grandfather will wait for you. He won't eat all the food."

Ellen entered the room as if going into a sacred church building. In the bedroom fireplace, a few logs burned. The portraits of George Washington and John Adams, the first two presidents, stared at her from the walls. Because Ellen's grandmother had died long ago, the room had a single bed, which fit into a little hollow space in the wall. It was put there to leave room for a small table, some chairs, and other bedroom furniture.

Grandfather and granddaughter ate a simple tea of bread, honey, and lettuce with a vinegar dressing. It had been brought to them on a tray by one of his dozen servants.

"Grandpapa," Ellen said in between bites of bread, "why did you cut up that New Testament?"

The president smiled and patted her hand. "It's sort of an experiment," he said. "I think that Jesus' words are very wise. I cut out all of His teachings. Then I put them together in a new book. I call it *The Life and Morals of Jesus*."

"Can you just do that?"

"Of course," he said. "It's my book. I wanted Jesus' good advice all together in one place. That's why I cut His words out."

It made sense to Ellen. She had often wanted to cut her favorite pictures out of some books so she wouldn't have to search through all the pages to find them. She wanted the best parts all in one spot.

"Now it is my turn for questions," he said. "What did you want a Bible for?"

"I was going to look in it for a clue to the riddle you gave me," she answered.

"There's no clue there, darling girl," he said. "You must figure out the puzzle by yourself. The secret is in knowing when to stop."

"I know!" cried Ellen. "It should read,

'I've seen the sea.

All in a blaze of fire, I've seen a house.

High as the moon and higher, I've seen the sun.

At twelve o'clock at night, I've seen the man who
saw this wondrous sight.'
You just have to know where to put the commas and the
periods."

"Yes," the president said. "That's one of the secrets of a
happy life. Knowing when to stop."

*   *   *   *   *

After tea, Ellen followed her grandfather downstairs. He
was going out for his usual horseback ride and was planning to take Jeff with him.

"Sorry," said Jeff as soon as he saw Ellen. "Deep down I
knew you wouldn't cut a book. I should have stood up for
you." Then he grinned. "But if Grandpa can cut up a book,
then I guess anyone could be guilty!" He waved good-bye as
he headed after the president, who had already left for the
stables where he kept his favorite horse, Wildair.

Ellen smiled and was glad to know there would be no
bad feelings. She had been fearful Jeff and Anne would be
jealous that she had been asked to join their grandfather.

When Ellen found Anne doing her sewing in her bedroom, Anne didn't tell Ellen that she was sorry. But that was
her way.

Ellen noticed that Anne had changed her hair. She still
had it swept up in curls on top of her head like Ellen's. But
she had fixed it differently on one side so a curl fell loose,
and a ribbon was tied in a bow above her ear.

"May I have the key to the library?" Ellen asked. "I want
to get my poem and the books I left in there."

"I suppose you may go alone. I want to sew. Here it is."
Anne took a gold chain from around her neck and

14

unclasped it. Then she dangled the key above Ellen's out-stretched palm.

"You must bring it right back," Anne demanded.

Ellen nodded, and Anne lowered the chain in a slow spiral. The gold necklace formed a circle-shaped pile in her hand, like a snake coiled up to strike.

Ellen clutched the chain and key in her palm and headed out of Anne's territory. She was surprised her sister had turned over the key so easily.

On the main floor of the President's House, Ellen put the key into the lock of the library door. She unlocked it and went inside. The sunny light from the south and west windows flooded the room and fell on the long table.

She gasped when she saw what was there. Jeff's squirrel skeleton was in pieces. The leg bones were on the floor, and the ribcage was split. A few of the neck bones were still stuck together.

She ran her fingers over the broken bits. *Who could have done this?* she asked herself. She picked up a bone fragment and held it up to the light from a window. Pegasus flapped from his cage to her shoulder.

She searched the room for clues. There were plenty of carpentry and garden tools lying around that could have been used to pull it apart. She picked up a hammer to see if it would have been heavy enough to crush the bones. She turned when she heard Anne's voice coming from the door. "What did you do to Jeff's skeleton?"

"I found it like this," Ellen said, looking at Anne. The older girl was holding back a mean smile.

"Don't act so innocent," Anne said. "You are holding a

15

hammer, you know. I caught you in the act."

"Why would I ruin Jeff's experiment?" Ellen asked.

Anne lifted her chin. "You did it to get back at Jeff for saying you cut the book."

"But I didn't get in trouble," said Ellen. "Why would I still be angry? And what were you doing down here any-way? I thought you wanted to sew."

"I changed my mind. Now I want to finish my letter to Emily." Anne grabbed her letter from the table and spun toward the door, her long dress swishing as she stalked out of the room. Ellen was left alone with the scattered bones and Pegasus.

She glanced around the room one more time. Everything else was just as they had left it. Or was it? Had her poem been folded in half? She couldn't remember. She would ask the servants if they had seen anyone enter the library.

If she couldn't find out who did it, Anne might accuse her. And this time, Ellen doubted that her grandfather was going to save her.

CHAPTER

3

Hide and Seek

The next morning at the breakfast table, Anne made an announcement. "Now that I'm almost fifteen," she said, "I would like it if everyone called me Anastasia."

Ellen had to look down at her plate of sugarcoated pancakes to keep from giggling. Jeff couldn't hold his laughter, and put a white linen napkin to his mouth. But his chuckles still shook the long table as his body rocked back and forth.

"Oh, Jeff," said Mrs. Randolph, "don't laugh at your sister so. When I was young, everyone called me Patsy. When I got older, they began to call me Martha. And you go by your middle name. Why shouldn't Anne want to be called something different?"

Anne's dark eyes flashed a look of victory, and she smiled. Ellen didn't like this change. It somehow made Anne seem older. Their mother was letting Anne grow up too fast.

Ellen said in a proud voice, "Anne is still only fourteen. If she gets to be Anastasia, then I'm Eleonora." She turned to her father, who was sitting on her right. "Daddy, may I be please be called Eleonora?"

Before the surprised Thomas Randolph had time to answer his daughter, the president spoke.

"*Anne,*" he said firmly, "when you and *Ellen* are finished with your breakfast, you will find a stack of books for you in your rooms."

The matter was settled. Their grandfather did not want them to change their names. He had sent a clear message that he did not approve of the names Anastasia and Eleonora.

Anne gave a big sigh and pushed her plate away. A servant quickly removed the dish. Breakfast was over. Thomas Randolph, a congressman, left for his office in the city. The president went into his study.

Ellen went upstairs to the family quarters and found the books her grandfather had chosen for her to read. A few French books, one on art, some poetry, and *The Life and Morals of Jesus* copied in her grandfather's own handwriting.

She grabbed the religious book. Her family did not go to church because her father, Thomas Randolph, did not like it. Her mother still prayed many of the prayers she had learned at a religious school in France. And Ellen had heard the slaves in Virginia talk a good bit about the miracles in the Old Testament. Though she believed in God, Ellen had never read the teachings of Jesus. Her grandfather's collection of Jesus' quotes didn't make a long book, and she had almost finished parts one and two when she heard a knock on her bedroom door.

It was Cornelia with wispy pale hair and a runny nose. "Will you play with me?" the child asked. "Mama, Mary, and Virginia are taking naps."

"Let me get my sweater," said Ellen. Many of the rooms of the President's House were not finished. Few fires burned to keep the rooms warm, so the children needed to wear heavy clothing when they were playing in the large, drafty rooms.

The girls went downstairs to play in the large Audience Room. It was not yet ready for guests to use as a ballroom. The president had put up a temporary wall at one end of the long room to use as a meeting place for his advisers. The Randolphs had turned the rest of it into a playroom, and their grandfather had filled the room with toys.

Ellen was too old for the rocking horse and blocks, and she got bored playing pretend with her sister. But Ellen loved to play hide-and-seek with Cornelia. "I'll cover my eyes first," Ellen said. "You may hide anywhere that's not locked."

At first Ellen looked in all the closets, but Cornelia wasn't in any of them. A peek inside the family dining room revealed Cornelia, who laughed when Ellen found her hiding underneath the table, with a cloth covering it. "My turn!" Cornelia squealed.

Ellen liked to hide behind the furniture in the oval-shaped room that faced the Potomac River. She lay down on a red sofa that had its back to the door and faced a window. Ellen looked outside while she waited for Cornelia to find her. During that time, she saw Jeff walk into the woods, a rifle tucked underneath his arm. He was slinking like a farm dog that had just stolen an egg from the hen house.

On the fourth round of the game, Ellen couldn't find Cornelia. She even checked the nursery and stairways.

Ellen widened her search to her grandfather's private rooms. She knocked on the study door. When no one answered, she tried the handle. It was unlocked. As she walked in, she noticed her things were still on the table next to the broken squirrel skeleton. But there was also a bunch of her grandfather's papers scattered across the table. The table was messier than usual.

Once more, Ellen ran her hand across the broken bones. The previous evening Anne had tried to convince Jeff that Ellen had ruined the squirrel skeleton. In answer, he had laughed.

"I won't falsely accuse Ellen again," said Jeff.

"She's not an angel or anything," argued Anne. "She wanted to get back at you for saying she cut the book. I saw her with a hammer."

"She didn't do it any more than she tore the Bible," Jeff answered.

"Then who did it?" asked Anne, fists rounded and resting on her narrow hips.

"I don't know," Jeff answered coolly. "But I'd believe that Pegasus did it before I'd believe bad of Ellen again."

At the thought of the mockingbird, Ellen looked over at the window. Pegasus' cage stood empty.

Ellen saw a movement near a wall. The bird sat perched atop some wooden rods with maps rolled around them. Ellen went slowly up to him and offered her finger as a perch. No sooner had Pegasus jumped aboard her finger than he fluttered over to a large cabinet built into the wall. He bobbed his head as if he were trying to say something.

"What is it, Mr. Pegasus?" Ellen asked. "What's in here?"

As Ellen touched the cabinet door, it sprang open. She heard a giggle.

"Cornelia!" Ellen cried. "What a good hiding spot!"

The six-year-old crawled out from the small cabinet. Inside was a tray and room for the president's midnight snack and drink. There were also treats for the bird: dried fruit and nuts.

"It sure is dark in there," Ellen said. "Weren't you frightened?"

Cornelia shook her head. "How did you find me?"

"Pegasus hopped over here," Ellen explained. "I never would have dreamed of opening Grandpapa's private cabinet without his permission. Now quick, let's put the bird back before we get into trouble. You aren't allowed in here."

Ellen carefully caught the gray mockingbird with both hands trapping his wings. His long legs dangled out between her fingers like dried twigs. After placing Pegasus gently back inside the cage, she shut the door. Then she gave the door an extra tug to make sure it was closed. Cornelia pushed a dried cherry inside the cage, and Pegasus quickly snapped it up in his beak.

As the girls left the study, the mockingbird sang a sweet song that reminded Ellen of spring. But it didn't take her mind off the question of who had left her grandfather's library door unlocked.

CHAPTER

4

Mrs. Smith's Bad News

Shortly before tea the next day, the girls were in Ellen's room, planning for the New Year's Day party at the President's House. Anne wanted her shadow portrait cut in case a gentleman should ask her for a keepsake.

Anne sat in a chair, her back straight as a fire poker. A candle on one side of her cast her shadow on the wall. Ellen held a piece of paper and was cutting out the shape of Anne's profile from a piece of black paper. Curled up scraps lay on the floor.

"Let me see it," Anne said. "I'm tired of sitting so still."

Ellen silently handed the portrait to Anne.

"My nose isn't so flat, is it?" Anne asked. "And my hair is much too big. Oh, I wish Mama would pay for a real artist to cut my portrait. You must try it again. This isn't good enough."

Ellen, who hadn't wanted to cut the profile in the first place, didn't say anything. She picked up a new sheet of paper and began to cut, starting at Anne's chin. This time, she made sure the nose was long and straight, even though

Anne's real nose was shorter and rounded.

As she worked, she thought of the book she had been reading the night before. "But love ye your enemies," Jesus had said, "and do good . . . hoping for nothing again; and your reward shall be great, and ye shall be the children of the Highest: for he is kind unto the unthankful and to the evil." Last night, the words had seemed wise and kind. After cutting Anne's profile for the fifth time, though, the words seemed difficult to live by. *Why must I love her when she isn't nice to me?* thought Ellen. *She surely is unthankful and mean.*

A knock at the door revealed the doorman, Jean Sioussant. He was a Frenchman, who had worked for a British official in the past. Ellen didn't know him very well, but he was in charge of everyone who entered the President's House. The servants and the president's grand-children called him "French John" because his name was so hard to pronounce.

"A Mrs. Samuel Harrison Smith is here to call," he announced. "I have asked her to wait in the drawing room."

"Mrs. Smith," cried Ellen, dropping the paper and scissors on her white candlewick bedspread. She practically flew down the hall and the staircase to the oval room. Anne quickly followed, not wanting to be left out.

Three years earlier, the Randolphs had met Mrs. Smith in Washington City. Ellen and Mrs. Smith had become good friends because they shared a love for poetry. When Ellen saw the well-dressed familiar woman she hugged her. Mrs. Smith's perfume smelled just like honeysuckle on a hot day.

If anyone was going to make a good impression by

wearing the right clothes, it was Mrs. Smith. Her collar was pleated and wide, circling her neck like a horse harness. Her white hat reminded Ellen of a turban, the feather sticking up making it look even more fashionable.

Mrs. Smith took a small package out of a large bag made from heavy material. She handed Ellen the box wrapped in shiny gold paper. Anne watched as Ellen's delicate hands tore at the covering and discovered a book of William Wordsworth's poems.

"Thank you," Ellen said. "It's beautiful. Wherever did you find it? Not even Grandpapa has this volume."

Anne looked at the book as if it were a child's toy that she had outgrown. "Perhaps he has read it," she said, "and decided that it's not worth owning."

At her sister's cruel words, Ellen sank on the sofa, clutching the book to her chest. She couldn't believe Anne had said something so rude in front of a guest.

"Well," said Mrs. Smith, trying not to sound annoyed, but failing. "I will let Ellen judge the worth of the book. She has a great ear for poetry."

For a few seconds, the two girls and the woman said nothing. Ellen stared out the window, watching the small ferries cross the Potomac. Finally Mrs. Smith broke the silence. She tried to make friends with Anne, even after Anne had been so rude. "I see you have the latest-style fabric," Mrs. Smith said. "Did you purchase that in Washington City?"

"We have no one to take us," Anne answered in a voice that Ellen recognized. It was the one her sister used to sound grown-up. "How could we go to the city with Mama in her fragile condition? Father works all the time, as does Grandpapa, now that Congress is in session."

"I see," was all Mrs. Smith said.

There was a longer silence this time. Ellen looked at the faces of the other two in the room. The older woman's was blank, as if she were trying to turn herself into a garden statue. Anne was looking out the window, playing with one of the curls that she let dangle on the side of her cheek.

The awful silence returned. Ellen forced herself to speak. "Did you come to see Grandpapa?" she asked Mrs. Smith. "I think he is in a meeting with one of his cabinet members in the study. We could all go in."

The woman and two girls stood at the same time. Ellen led the way out of the room and into the study, which had an open door.

The president and Mrs. Smith greeted each other like the comfortable friends they were. One of the president's advisers bowed to the lady and two girls, then he left.

"I wasn't going to say this in front of the children," Mrs. Smith said. "But I've changed my mind. They are old enough to hear it."

She pulled a newspaper out from inside the big carpet-bag she carried. With a quick snap of her wrist, she opened the paper. "This is not from my husband's paper, mind you. He was offered the story, but he turned it down. He didn't think any reasonable newspaper would print it. It seems he was wrong. Very wrong. This story is all over Boston, too."

Mrs. Smith took a deep breath and began to read, "The title is 'Hide Your Bibles.' 'The president has taken to cutting up the Holy Scriptures. Christians, beware, the day is coming when Thomas Jefferson will make reading the Bible a crime. Hide your Sacred Texts! The God-hater is out to destroy them.'"

Ellen's stomach lurched as if it were full of bacon grease. She loved and respected her grandfather. Hearing the lies written in the newspaper made her feel sick. The papers in Virginia didn't say such things about her grandfather.

Ellen didn't want to hear any more lies. She put her hands over her ears and rushed out of the study and up to the safety of her room.

CHAPTER

5

The Key

Not long after Mrs. Smith left, Jeff, Anne, and Ellen were gathered into the president's study, with the door firmly shut. Thomas Jefferson sat in a wooden chair with a tapestry covering. The children sat around the table as they had the day before. The broken bones reminded Ellen of a grave-yard, for she knew they were going to hear bad news.

"I don't know how," the president said, "but someone found out about my little experiment with the New Testament. Besides myself, there are only three other people who knew I had taken apart the words of Christ. Now, it seems, anyone can read about it in the newspaper."

"But—" Anne began.

Thomas Jefferson waved his hand to cut her off. "No, don't say anything yet," he said. "The newspapers have been calling me a Christian-hater for years. It is nothing new. I do not attend church on a regular basis; that is no secret. But I would never stop anyone from going to a church. And I would never destroy someone's religious books. But newspapers print what they want to. It is useless to defend myself."

"But why?" asked Ellen. "It's all lies!"

"Even the Bible says to bear it when people say bad things about you," he said. "It's just part of life."

He folded his hands and gently placed them in his lap. He looked at each grandchild with his hazel eyes. "Now, suppose you tell me how someone might have found out about my Bible experiment."

Jeff was first to speak. "Would any of the servants tell?"

"One or two might have," said the president. "I have thought of it. But only one special servant is allowed in my study to clean and bring me food. And he does not know how to read. He wouldn't know a Bible from a cookbook. Did any of you mention the book to anyone at all?"

Jeff, Anne, and Ellen shook their heads no.

The Life and Morals of Jesus has been on my nightstand," said Ellen. "Perhaps someone saw it there."

"I thought of that, too," said the president. "But that is the neat copy. It has no loose or torn pages. I carefully pasted it with my own hand. No one would describe it as torn or ruined."

The grandchildren could offer no more information. Ellen wondered if Jeff had talked to anyone when he sneaked out to go hunting. But she decided not to mention it in case he got in trouble.

There were two things bothering Ellen, and she wanted her grandfather to know about them. "Grandpapa," she said, "there is also Jeff's ruined skeleton. Someone came in while everybody else was having tea."

Anne rolled her eyes. "We all know that you did it, Ellen.

Why not confess?"

Ellen held back the angry words she wanted to say. She would not fight back against lies. The truth would win out. She glanced at her grandfather, who gave her a wink. The look in his eyes said, "Good girl for keeping quiet!"

"I've got something else to mention," said Ellen. "Yesterday morning Cornelia and I were playing hide-and-seek. She hid in here. The door must have been unlocked for her to get in."

"Did she touch anything?" the president asked. "I have many valuables in here."

"Just Pegasus," she answered. "And she hid in the cabinet."

The president slowly shook his gray-haired head. "I'm sorry, children," he said, "but I can't allow you to play in here anymore. There are federal secrets kept here. Some of my maps and papers could get us into a war with Spain if the newspapers published them. My enemies, especially Aaron Burr, would love to know what my plans are. If newspapers found out about the Bible, they can find out about anything."

He turned to Anne. "I must ask for the key back."

Anne's lower lip began to quiver. Then it curled down like a wilted rose petal. After unclasping the gold chain and sliding the key off of it, she laid the key gently on the table. As if knowing that they were dismissed, all three children stood and slowly walked out of the study.

As soon as they were in the hallway with the door shut behind them, Anne hissed, "It's all your fault, Ellen. Why did you have to tell him about the unlocked door? I never went into the library yesterday."

"Then who did?" Ellen asked.

"How should I know?" Anne replied. Then she left, her elfish chin pointed in the air.

"What's with her anyway?" Jeff asked. "She seems out to get you these days."

"I don't know," Ellen replied. "If I've done something to hurt her, I don't know what it is. I wish I could fix it. It's not easy having an enemy for a sister."

CHAPTER

Search in the Dark

Ellen woke when hot wax dripped on her hand.

But she couldn't scream. Someone's hand was covering her mouth.

The melted wax came from a single candle resting in a brass candlestick. The light from it lit up the corner of the bedroom. Ellen let out one long breath when she saw who was holding the candle: Jeff.

"Sorry about the wax," he whispered, taking his hand off of her mouth. "It was an accident. I didn't mean to startle you. But there really is no nice way to wake up someone at two in the morning."

"What are you doing here?" she asked, rubbing the spot on her hand where the wax had dripped.

"Put on your slippers and come with me," he said. "I want to find out what has been going on in Grandpa's study."

"Did you wake Anne?"

"No," he laughed. "I want someone I can trust. Come on."

Jeff chose the narrow, twisty servant's staircase. Ellen followed his long wool shirt and bare feet. With white petticoat and pantalets, she made a pale, glowing figure as the candlelight reflected off her clothes. If anyone had been watching, the two Randolphs would have looked like ghosts.

"I'm glad we left our dog at home," Jeff whispered. "If he were here, he'd be barking so loud he'd wake the city."

At the heavy wooden door to the study, Jeff handed Ellen the candle. "Here, hold this," he said. "I need you to shine the light right on the doorknob."

Ellen watched as Jeff pushed a bent, flattened nail into the lock.

"What's that?" she asked.

"Shh."

He twisted the nail just twice. Then he turned the knob. The door swung open.

"How did you do that?" Ellen insisted on knowing.

"I learned that trick from one of the slaves back home," Jeff explained. "I won't say which one, so you can't snitch on him."

"Do the slaves steal from us?"

"Not really. But sometimes if the overseer is treating them bad, they take what they need to live."

Ellen stared at her brother in amazement. How did he know so much? He was only thirteen.

Jeff fiddled with the doorknob some and kept putting in and taking out the bent, thin nail. "Just like I thought," he said. "It's simple to open. But it's almost impossible to lock without a key. Whoever has been getting in has been picking the lock. But when he—or she—leaves, the door is left unlocked. That's a clue."

"Why do you think someone has been sneaking in here?" Ellen asked. The President's House had seemed so safe before.

"One," he answered, "my ruined skeleton. Since you didn't do it, someone else must have."

Ellen nodded in agreement.

"Two," Jeff continued, "you found the door unlocked yesterday when you and Cornelia played hide-and-seek. Three, someone read Anne's letter. That's how the newspaper got the story."

Ellen's eyes opened as round as a harvest moon. Even with only the low glow from the candle, Jeff could tell she was shocked.

"I didn't really snoop," Jeff explained. "Anne wanted me to add a note to Emily's brother at the bottom of the letter. I couldn't help but read that she wrote all about how funny it was for Grandpa to cut up a book—and that she thinks you ruined my skeleton."

Ellen stomped her foot. It didn't make much noise because of her soft slippers and the thick carpet on the floor, but it felt good. "How could she say that I did it? That's not fair. It isn't true. And why didn't Anne tell Grandpapa about the letter she wrote?"

"I can't tell what's going on with Anne these days," Jeff said. "If she is just acting like a lady, I hope you never become one."

"Maybe she just didn't think of it," Ellen said, not ready to believe Anne would lie to their grandfather.

"Anyway," Jeff said to change the subject, "don't tell

anyone, not even Anne, that you know about her letter to her friend, okay?"

Ellen agreed. As the brother and sister sneaked back to their bedrooms, one other bedroom door was open just a crack. A pair of angry brown eyes watched Jeff and Ellen go inside their rooms.

CHAPTER

7

Aaron Burr

Mrs. Smith called at the President's House just after tea the next day. She found all the Randolph children in the Audience Room. The president was down on the floor with Virginia and Mary. He pretended to be their horse.

"If the people could see you now," Mrs. Smith said to Thomas Jefferson, "they would never suppose you to be a devil. I wish you would write a defense of yourself. My husband will be so glad to print it."

"What for?" asked the president, standing. "My friends know me and don't believe the lies. My enemies wouldn't believe the truth anyway."

Ellen listened and realized that her grandfather was taking the advice of Jesus again. Before she had fallen asleep, she had been thinking about Anne's lies. She recalled Jesus' words, "Blessed are ye, when men . . . shall say all manner of evil against you falsely, for my sake. Rejoice and be exceeding glad: for great is your reward in heaven."

Ellen couldn't be happy that Anne was spreading lies. But she knew that it would do no good to defend herself.

Truth would win, even if she had to wait until heaven.

"Well, Ellen," said Mrs. Smith. "May I take you to the city? I have a few things I must pick up for my house in the country. I should be glad of your company."

Anne had been sitting in the corner. She was sewing and listening, but Mrs. Smith did not ask her to come. Ellen whispered in Mrs. Smith's ear; she asked Mrs. Smith to invite Anne. The look Mrs. Smith gave Ellen said, "Are you sure you want *her* along?"

Ellen nodded. She wanted to do good to her sister.

"Anne," said Mrs. Smith, with a kind smile, "I will want your expert advice on some fabric I am going to purchase. Will you please come with us? I understand you are good with making clothes."

Anne smiled and nodded. She was pleased to be asked as one lady to another.

The president gave each of the girls a half-dollar to spend. He also loaned them his driver, his carriage, and his four matching horses. To be able to ride in such a fine carriage was a treat for the girls.

They rode away from the Potomac River and down Pennsylvania Avenue. Some of the potholes in the street had been filled, and there wasn't as much mud as usual for that time of year. The poplar trees, planted at the wishes of Thomas Jefferson, grew on either side of the avenue and fanned at them as they passed. Ellen felt as though she was in a parade and the tall trees were waving to her.

Anne was her happy self. She was acting like the friend and sister that Ellen so wanted. *I'm glad we invited Anne*, she thought.

"We'll get a new hanky for Mother and some candy for the girls," suggested Anne. "And a whistle for Jeff. He left his back in Virginia."

They passed the rows of small houses built for the congressmen and their families and other people living in the federal city. Despite a few large inns and a sturdy church or two, the city was still farmlike. The girls and Mrs. Smith passed by more cows than they did horses. Neat rows of trees that formed orchards lined the countryside.

"I need to go straight to the stagecoach. I've a letter to send by today's post," Mrs. Smith advised the coachman.

The post driver was dressed in a heavy brown jacket, with a scarf around his neck. He asked Mrs. Smith, "Are those the president's grandchildren I see with you?"

"Yes. Misses Ellen and Anne Randolph."

"Where's Miss Anastasia?"

Before Mrs. Smith could find an answer, the man gave a shout. "Can't wait. The post must not be slow!" With a snap of the reins he held in his muscular, tan hands, the horses thundered off.

"Anastasia?" Mrs. Smith asked, looking back and forth at Ellen then at Anne. "Who is Anastasia?"

"He must have been confused," Ellen said. "But to herself she thought, *How odd that he should guess at Anne's dream name.*

As the carriage slowed in front of the store, Mrs. Smith apologized. "This store is nowhere near as nice as the one in Baltimore. But it will have to do for today."

The coachman helped Mrs. Smith and the Randolph girls out of the carriage. They stepped into the store filled

with barrels and wooden shelves. The store had everything
from pipes to peanuts, flower bulbs to fabric. Ellen loved the
smells the best: the rich smell of coffee mixed with cinnamon
tea and pine soap. When she whiffed the chocolate, it was
almost as if she could feel it melt against her tongue.

The girls selected their things. Ellen had a difficult time
choosing between candied orange peels and licorice for the
girls. Anne selected a white lace hanky for their mother.

Mrs. Smith purchased a rich yellow material for her curtains. "I want these to look like the green curtains in the
president's dining room," said Mrs. Smith. "Your grandfather had those made. They're a light new fabric from
France."

They strolled down the street toward the hat shop. "I
want a new hat for the New Year's Party," said Mrs. Smith.
"Everyone dresses up for it. If you want to be noticed, you
have to have a grand hat."

And Mrs. Smith did want to be noticed. Off to the hat
shop the three shoppers went.

An older man came out of an inn and walked toward
them. "My goodness," said Mrs. Smith. "That's Aaron Burr."
He was balding in the front, but still wore his brown hair
long in back as was the style. He looked formal in his dark
jacket with long tails and black shoes with silver buckles.

The girls froze. Aaron Burr's name gave Ellen a weird
feeling in her stomach. Aaron Burr and Thomas Jefferson
had both wanted to be president in 1800. The girls' grandfather had won by a single vote.

Mr. Burr had then served as vice president for one term.
During the next term, Jefferson did not ask Mr. Burr to be

vice president. That made Mr. Burr angry. He felt that President Jefferson was trying to ruin his life.

Ellen slowed her steps. "Can't we go back to the carriage? I don't want to look at new hats after all."

"We can't be mean to him. The president wouldn't like it," said Mrs. Smith. "He wants Mr. Burr to be treated well. The president even invited him over for dinner last month."

That's right, thought Ellen. *We must be good to our enemies.*

Mr. Burr bowed to the girls and Mrs. Smith. He said he had a meeting to attend, and so he passed quickly.

"That was strange," said Mrs. Smith. "He is usually friendly. We often have a nice long chat."

"Didn't he kill Alexander Hamilton?" Anne whispered after Mr. Burr was out of sight.

"He was in a duel with Mr. Hamilton," Mrs. Smith said. "Mr. Hamilton was wounded and later died. The duel destroyed Mr. Burr's chance at holding any public office."

"Why did Mr. Burr challenge Mr. Hamilton to a duel?" asked Ellen.

"Mr. Burr didn't like some things that Mr. Hamilton said about him in public. Mr. Hamilton also paid to have bad stories written about Mr. Burr," she said. "The newspapers printed those stories, and a lot of people believed them."

"Then," Anne said, "Mr. Burr was defending his honor, that is all. That's not so bad. I wish Grandpapa would fight back, too."

"But to kill a man!" cried Ellen. "What is honorable about that?"

"What should Mr. Burr have done?" challenged Anne. "Alexander Hamilton was spreading lies."

"Mr. Burr should have acted more like Grandpapa," said Ellen. "If he had ignored the lies, Mr. Hamilton would be alive. As it is now, Mr. Burr is laughed at in the streets. Is that so honorable?"

Ellen had spoken with such fierceness that even Mrs. Smith didn't know what to say. The soft pink of Ellen's cheeks had turned cherry red and spread across her face. Her hazel eyes flashed such emotion that a mother bear couldn't have shown such fury.

The rest of the shopping trip the girls and Mrs. Smith talked about chickens, pie crust, and French fashion. Nothing more was said about Aaron Burr.

CHAPTER

The Unlocked Door

"I can't find Cornelia," said Ellen to Anne the next afternoon, not long after tea. "I need help."

"Go ask Jeff," Anne said. "I'm busy fixing a dress for the New Year's party." She was in her bedroom with all eight branches of a candelabra lit to see the fine stitches she was making.

"Jeff's out with Grandpapa," said Ellen. "Everyone knows they go riding every day at one o'clock."

"Did you ask Mother to help?" Anne asked.

"Her back hurts," Ellen patiently explained. "The baby will come any day now. Besides, she can't see very well. She'd walk right past Cornelia."

"What about the servants?" Anne didn't look up from her sewing.

"Most of the servants are too busy preparing for the New Year's party," Ellen answered. "They have gone as far as Richmond to buy food. Some are baking, or cleaning, or setting up tables, or something."

"Try again without me." Anne was squinting at the

delicate pattern she was creating on the bodice of her nicest dress. "It should be simple to find her. She's only six."

"But she's small," Ellen said. "She can hide anywhere." Ellen feared that her sister had grown up so much that she would not help.

"Oh, all right," Anne said. She stabbed the needle into a pincushion. She put aside the dress and stood up.

"Have you checked the water closet?" suggested Anne. "She loves it in there because we have to use the outhouse when we're at home."

"It was the first place I looked."

They looked in the family bedchambers and the Audience Room with all the toys. They searched the family dining room. Anne looked in the servant's quarters while Ellen checked the kitchen in the basement. They asked three servants if they had seen Cornelia, including French John, the doorman. Then the sisters went through the halls and checked underneath all the sofas.

"There's only one place left," said Anne. "The study."

"Let's just try the door," said Ellen. "If it's locked, then she can't be there."

"You stand lookout," said Anne. "I don't want anyone watching us try to get in here. Grandpapa told the whole household we weren't to go inside."

Anne grabbed the doorknob. She gave it a gentle twist. It turned.

"Unlocked again!" Ellen said. "Cornelia must be in here."

The door swung open, and the Randolph girls looked inside. Anne let out a small gasp. Instead of Cornelia, there stood Aaron Burr.

42

Their grandfather's enemy was alone in the study with heaps of papers on the table. Cabinets doors hung open. And Pegasus perched on his finger. Mr. Burr stood inside the room as if he owned the President's House.

Ellen quickly shut the door. "Hurry," she whispered, "Go get French John. We can't let Mr. Burr leave without knowing why he is here alone in Grandpapa's private study."

Anne lifted her long dress so that her pantalets showed to the knees. Then she hurried down the hall, calling, "French John! French John!"

Ellen watched through the keyhole as Mr. Burr flicked Pegasus off of his finger. Next he shuffled through the papers on the table, stuffing a few of them into the pocket inside his jacket. He rolled up one map and put it underneath his arm.

"You must excuse me," Aaron Burr said after opening the door. He rushed past Ellen, who stood watching. She could do nothing to stop this man from stealing the map. He could have put anything else he wanted into his pockets. She stood in shock, as if she had just seen the sun fall from the sky.

In the hallway, Mr. Burr turned east. And while he didn't exactly run, he moved fast. Ellen had never seen a man of his age hurry like that inside a house.

Ellen followed him as he turned right into the formal dining room where the president had his fancy dinners.

Yes! Ellen thought. *He's trapped now. There's no other door.*

Anne and French John came hurrying down the hall. Their feet making soft thuds on the carpets.

"Over here," Ellen called. "He's in the dining room."

French John pushed open the door.

Inside stood Cornelia Randolph. Tears dribbled down her cheeks, wisps of her thin hair sticking to the moisture.

Aaron Burr had vanished.

CHAPTER

9

Cornelia's Story

Ellen rushed to Cornelia and took her into her arms. "What happened?" Ellen asked the six year old.

The only answer Ellen got was more sobs. French John took a hanky out of his pocket. He squatted down and gave it to Cornelia. She blew her nose, but tears still glided down her face. After a minute, her breathing slowed.

"I was hi-hiding in the cabinet," she said, still not quite calm. "And I fell a-asleep waiting for Ellen to find me."

French John went over to the cabinet. There were four pieces of wood on the floor about two feet wide and four feet long. He spun the door. "Of course!" he cried. "These are special cabinets built by the president. They open into the drawing room. That way the servants don't have to come in here when the president has guests. The servants load the food on the shelves. Next they spin the entire cabinet, and the food appears here."

He spun the cabinet. "Look," he said, pointing to the boards on the floor. "Mr. Burr removed the shelves on this side so that he could fit." Then French John got inside the cabinet. Using the wall to push off, he spun the large cabinet door and vanished. Like Aaron Burr, he had gone through a revolving door into the drawing room.

"Everyone knew about those special doors," Anne said to Ellen. "How come you let him go?"

"But I didn't know," said Ellen. "I'm not old enough to eat at Grandpapa's dinners. I have never seen those shelves spin."

Ellen put her arms around Cornelia. "That mean man woke you up and took you out of the cabinet, didn't he?"

Cornelia, weeping again, nodded then pressed her face into Ellen's shoulder.

"Come on, little girl" Ellen said. "You need a nap or a spanking. I don't know which."

Ellen had barely led her sister to the door when the president and Jeff came into the dining room.

"What in the world is going on?" asked President Jefferson. "Mr. Sioussant says that Aaron Burr was here."

Cornelia pushed Ellen away and ran to her grandfather. As soon as she was in her grandfather's arms, she began crying anew.

"No, no," he said. "We must not cry!" Then he tossed her into the air. Her pink-and-white striped dress flew up and her lacy pantalets and slip showed as she came down into his arms. With her blond hair flying, Cornelia looked like a cottonwood seed spinning in the wind.

"More! More!" Cornelia squealed.

Up again and again, Thomas Jefferson tossed Cornelia. Each time she came down, she was laughing harder. Ellen remembered those special days when she had been small enough for her grandfather to throw her into the air willy-nilly. Once, she too would have had every tear wiped away by their kind grandfather. She would have been bounced on his knee. Kissed goodnight. Given extra butter mints. Loved beyond measure.

Now that she was nine, Ellen was still loved. But the love didn't come in the form of fun games and hugs. Now she got books. Her grandfather paid for her art lessons. He taught her how to raise flowers and chickens. She recited French poetry to make him smile. She played the pianoforte to please him.

Jeff came over to her, still smelling of horses, and asked what had excited French John so much.

"It was just as you thought," Ellen explained. "The library door was unlocked again. Aaron Burr was inside looking at Grandfather's papers."

"Then he came when Grandpa was gone," Jeff said. "Mr. Burr knows the house and Grandpa's schedule. He could hide and wait for a good time to sneak into the library."

"He won't be allowed in again, of course," Ellen said. "That will solve the unlocked door mystery. Maybe Grandpapa will let us into the study again."

"Not so fast," Jeff said. "We still don't know who told the newspapers about the ruined Bible. Anne wrote that part of the letter in her room. The letter was never in the study after that."

"And there's the skeleton," Ellen said. "The door was locked the day I found it torn apart. I had to borrow Anne's key. Aaron Burr couldn't have done it."

"I already told you: Ellen did it." It was Anne's voice. She had come up behind them. "What are you two up to, anyway? I saw you both sneaking around in Grandpapa's study two nights ago. I think he should know about it."

*   *   *   *   *

There wasn't enough time for the president to hear Anne's story because he had to get ready for an important dinner.

"We'll talk about it later," he said to Anne, Jeff, and Ellen, "after I find out if Mr. Burr ran off with anything important."

For dessert that night, Ellen was given a snowball to eat. At least that is what she thought the creamy white mound was. She whispered to the servant who had been left in charge of the children, "Mammy, I think the chef forgot to heat this dessert. It's still cold."

The slave chuckled. "It's called ice cream," she said. "Mr. Jefferson brought back the recipe from France. Pick up your spoon and try it."

The good taste of the ice cream cheered Ellen. Once again, her mother, father, Jeff, and Anne had been invited to eat at a special dinner the president was having for some guests from Holland. Ellen didn't like to be left out. She thought she would enjoy hearing what the grown-ups talked about.

After Ellen had been in bed half an hour, her mother came in to kiss her goodnight. When Mrs. Randolph had gone, Ellen put down *The Life and Morals of Jesus*. She was just about to pinch out her candle and go to sleep when she heard a knock on the door.

"Come in," she called.

Jeff came in, still wearing the tight-fitting suit his mother made him wear to all formal dinners. Ellen thought he looked like a tin soldier because he moved so stiffly.

He took off the striped jacket with trim around the cuffs and sat on her bed.

"You should have seen it," he said. "There was a Dutch official at dinner. His head is as bald and shiny as the knob on your bedpost." Jeff rubbed his hand on the polished and rounded wood.

"The dessert pudding was too hot," Jeff continued. "While it was cooling on the plate, the Dutchman dropped his napkin. As he bent down to pick it up, his head hit the plate. The plate tipped over, and the hot pudding spilled all over his head."

Jeff began to laugh, and Ellen hit him with a pillow. "Go on," she said. "What happened?"

"He yelled out, 'My hair is on fire! My hair is on fire!' "

Ellen began to laugh too. And soon her door opened a crack. Anne's dark eyes peered in.

Ellen didn't want her sister to come in, but she remembered that she had to love her enemies. She motioned for her sister to enter.

Anne sat quietly at the foot of Ellen's bed. She was in no mood to laugh. "Someone has been reading my personal letters," she said. "And they are being printed in the newspaper. Which one of you has been stealing my letters?"

CHAPTER

Anastasia Again

"Why do you think that we've been stealing your letters?" asked Ellen.

Anne turned to Jeff. "Do you remember the Dutch official asking Grandpapa about the article in today's newspaper?"

Jeff nodded. "He read a bit of it just before the pudding spilled."

"Right," agreed Anne. "The newspaper said that Grandfather had been glad when Alexander Hamilton was shot and that he asked Aaron Burr to do it."

Ellen shivered. The lies gave her the chills even though she was under the covers.

"So?" asked Jeff.

"So, parts of it were in the exact same words as my letter. And then there was the cut up Bible. At first I didn't think it was possible that the newspapers got my letter ... but now ..."

"Did you really think Grandpa was happy that Mr. Hamilton was killed?" Jeff asked, his voice letting out a little of the anger he felt.

"No," Anne said. "But I wrote all about the duel. The

article was so much like my letter it scared me."

"Why do you think it was us?" Jeff asked.

"Because you took the first letter to the stagecoach. You could have given it to a newspaper," Anne snapped. "And Ellen was so upset about Aaron Burr's duel, I thought she might have given the second letter to her friend Mrs. Smith."

"Anne," said Ellen, not in the least upset at being blamed, "did you sign the letter 'Anastasia'?"

"See!" Anne said. "You did read it. I just started using the name Anastasia in my letters."

Ellen shook her head, moving her loose hair that glowed the color of fall maple leaves. "I didn't read it, but I know who did!"

Even Jeff was surprised at this. "Who?" he asked.

"The stagecoach driver," Ellen said plainly. "All letters go through him. Remember when he asked Mrs. Smith where Anastasia was? How would he know that name unless he read your letter?"

"Now we just need to know what happened to the skeleton," Jeff said. "Then all the mysteries will be solved."

"Ellen did it, Jeff. I saw her," Anne sighed. "Anyway, I'm going to tell Grandpapa about the letters. I feel so awful that I was the one who started the whole mess with the cut-up Bible."

All three Randolphs decided to go down to the study. Almost every night between six and ten o'clock, Thomas Jefferson worked in his library. He wrote letters, kept records of money spent, read books, and listened to Pegasus sing.

When Anne, Ellen, and Jeff entered, the president asked them to sit down. "Come in," he said. "I've been waiting for you. Anne was just about to burst this afternoon when I couldn't talk to her." He sat back in his chair and clasped his hands together, his first fingers still straight. He pointed them at his chin and watched his grandchildren.

This time none of the children wanted to speak. Ellen finally felt brave enough to dive in. "Anne was going to tell you that Jeff and I sneaked down here a few nights ago."

"What were you looking for at night that you couldn't find during the day?" Mr. Jefferson asked.

Jeff answered. "It was my idea. I wanted to see if we could pick the lock. Then we would know if someone else could do it and lock the door again."

"And what did you find?" asked Thomas Jefferson.

"That you can't lock it," Jeff said. "I'm sorry I didn't ask. But I didn't want you to know that I could pick locks." He took the nail out of his pocket and put it on the table in front of his grandfather. The president picked up the nail and studied it closely.

"What else?" the wise man asked, suddenly looking up.

"I didn't tell you that I wrote Emily about the Bible," Anne said. "When you asked us if we had told anyone, I kept quiet."

There was silence in the room. Anne swallowed several times before going on. Fear was blocking her throat.

Anne told him all about the other letter, the name Anastasia, and the stagecoach driver. The whole time the president just nodded his head. He wasn't frowning, but he wasn't smiling either.

"I wish you had told me sooner. Next time," he said, "give your letters to me. I have a special servant to carry my letters."

"Thank you," Anne said. She was glad that she hadn't gotten in trouble. It was bad enough knowing that her grandfather was disappointed.

"Is there anything else?" the president asked his grandchildren.

"Yes," Ellen said. "Did Mr. Burr take anything important?"

"Yes and no," said the president. "He got some maps that I will have to redraw. He also took copies of letters I wrote to my friends in Spain. But I don't think he can get us into a war. If he turns them over to the newspapers, then there will be some more lies. But that is all."

This time Jeff had a question. "Do you think Mr. Burr took apart my skeleton?"

At this, the president laughed. "You still haven't figured that out yet?"

"I have," said Anne, suddenly angry. "I saw Ellen in here with that hammer." Anne pointed at the tool still on the table near the bones. "She must have done it."

Ellen wanted to speak out, but she knew better. She waited for her grandfather to say something.

"Anne," he said, "you told me that Ellen had cut up my book, and she hadn't. Hold your tongue."

"But this time I saw her!" Anne said. "Ellen did it! She's not the angel everyone thinks she is."

"You saw her holding a hammer," the president explained. "But not hurting the skeleton. Ellen did not do it."

Anne looked at the green carpet on the floor. She was too mad to look up at her grandfather. She kicked a chair with her high-heeled lace-up boot.

Jeff asked, "Then who did? It's been driving me crazy."

The president smiled. "Pegasus," he said.

As if knowing what was being said, the bird flew to the table. He picked up a bone in his beak and hopped across the room. He landed on top of a bookcase and dropped the bone.

"But why?" asked Jeff. "And how?"

"I've noticed that Pegasus has been getting out of his cage," the president said. "You aren't the only one who knows how to pick a lock. And mockingbirds don't like strangers in their homes. He probably attacked the skeleton before the glue dried. He just tore it apart."

"Now we can get some sleep," Ellen said. "All of the mysteries are solved."

"You and Jeff may go," the president said. "But Anne and I need to talk."

Anne simply sat in her chair, staring at the bone Pegasus had dropped.

As Ellen crawled into bed for the second time that night, she worried about Anne. Ellen had thought that she wanted her sister to get into trouble. But now that it had happened, Ellen wasn't happy. Ellen believed that her grandfather was going to punish her sister for falsely accusing her. She hoped Anne's punishment wasn't going to be bad.

Several minutes later, Anne came upstairs. She slammed her door closed. But even with the door shut, Ellen heard her sister sobbing long into the night.

CHAPTER

11

The New Year's Party

The party was to start at two o'clock. Mrs. Smith came early to see about the girls. Ellen came downstairs at once to greet her friend.

"You look lovely, Ellen. But where is Anne?" Mrs. Smith asked. Her new hat was a huge green twist of fabric with peacock feathers sticking out of it. "I know she has been decorating a dress especially for this party. I want to be the first to see it."

"She won't come out of her room," Ellen said. "And she hasn't answered my knocks. I've slipped six letters underneath her door, and still she won't come out. She missed breakfast and tea."

The friends went through the rooms on the main floor. Several tables were set up with all sorts of cakes. The president's French chef had created so many different kinds, Ellen wasn't sure she would know which kind to eat first.

Her mother joined them wearing a wig as white and curly as lamb's wool. She did not look like a simple country woman, but a rich lady. Mrs. Randolph wore a long dress with a short waist. It had a poof in front where the baby was, but the style was flattering. "Oh, there's the British diplomat," Mrs. Randolph said. "I must begin greeting the guests."

The Marine Corps band was set up in the middle of the oval drawing room. A trumpet sounded and the lively music rang through the house. But the music didn't fill Ellen with cheer.

She had figured out what Anne's punishment was to be: no party. Hadn't that been Anne's own plan for Ellen when the book had been found torn?

Ellen picked up four pieces of cake and squeezed them all onto one plate. She took three of them to the nursery: one for Mammy, one for Cornelia, and one for Virginia and Mary to split.

She took the last piece to Anne. The bedroom door was open, and her grandfather was sitting on the bed next to her sister.

The president stood when she entered. He wore a plain black suit. His shoes were as simple: no buckle. He gave Ellen a grandfatherly hug and said, "You look so pretty, my dear."

Ellen glanced at Anne. She had never seen her sister look so unlovely. Puffy red lids surrounded her dark eyes so that she looked like a chicken. One side of her hair was in curls; the other side was straight. Her tears had soaked into it and washed away the curls. She was still only in her petticoat and pantalets.

"I've brought you both New Year's gifts," their grandfather said.

Only then did Ellen notice the packages on the night table. By the size and shape of the boxes, Ellen could tell what the gifts were. One was a hat, the other a book.

He gave Anne the hatbox. For all her sadness, Anne brightened at the idea of the gift. Quickly her fingers untied the string. She lifted off the box lid and pulled out a leghorn hat with silk roses around the rim. She perched the straw hat atop her head and looked into a mirror.

"Thank you, Grandpapa," she said. "It will be the prettiest hat in all of Virginia. I can't wait until Emily sees it."

Ellen's turn was next. She put down the cake plate on Anne's chest of drawers. She unwrapped a Bible. The sturdy brown leather cover was smooth underneath her fingers.

"Now don't cut this one up," her grandfather warned.

Ellen smiled and gave him another hug. "Shouldn't you be greeting the guests?" she asked. "After all, everyone comes to see you."

"The thousands come to be admired and to admire their friends," he said. "They also want to see how I've decorated the President's House. And this year your mother is here. But I do want to meet with the Indian chiefs when they come. I've been practicing my Cherokee. I hope to try out some new phrases."

He paused and held out his elbow, "May I escort you to the party, Ellen?"

"No," said Ellen. "But will you take Anne? I'll stay here in her place."

Thomas Jefferson paused and said, "That's your choice. If Anne agrees to let you take her punishment, I'll wait five minutes for her to get ready." Their grandfather left the room.

Anne turned to Ellen. "But what about my hair? It looks like a bird made a nest in one side."

"Just put it up underneath your new hat," Ellen said. "No one will notice."

Anne jumped off the bed. "The dress is finished. Oh, Ellen, will you polish my shoes?"

"I'll clean them the best I can in four minutes," she said.

In less than three, Anne was on her grandfather's arm and heading to the party.

Just for a second, Ellen wondered why she had let Anne go to the party when her sister did deserve to miss it for spreading lies. But when she opened the Bible and read what her grandfather had written, she knew she had done the right thing.

In his fine handwriting Thomas Jefferson had penned:

"January 1, 1806

To Ellen Wayles Randolph:

'And as ye would that men should do to you, do ye also unto them likewise.'

The words of Jesus from Luke 6:31.

With love always,

Grand Papa"

Did You Know?

Martha Jefferson Randolph and her six children visited Thomas Jefferson at the President's House (now called the White House) from December 2, 1805 to May 9, 1806. While Aaron Burr did not rob the president's library, many of the other events in this story are true, including the following:

• Thomas Jefferson penned the riddle on page five. But it was not given to Ellen. The riddle was sent to Cornelia Jefferson Randolph when she was eight.

• In 1805, Jefferson was collecting New Testaments in various languages.

• During his second term as president, Thomas Jefferson edited *The Life and Morals of Jesus of Nazareth*, a compilation of the New Testament teachings of Jesus. He cut up a complete set of the Gospels to make the book. There is no evidence that anyone else knew of the existence of the book until some years later when he kept it by his bedside.

• When he was young, Thomas Jefferson built model skeletons from bones he found in the woods.

• At some point in her youth, Ellen Wayles Randolph

received a Bible from Thomas Jefferson. It was one of the gifts from him that she treasured the most.

• Aaron Burr was in the Washington City area in late 1805, and he dined with the president that November. Burr hoped the United States would go to war with Spain. With the president fighting a foreign country, Burr would be free to gain control of the new Western territories. He eventually wanted to take over the United States and make himself president.

• Thomas Jefferson kept pet mockingbirds at the President's House. He let them roam freely in his library when he was there. They ate food from his lips and followed him when he left the library.

• In 1805, Anne and Ellen both wanted to change their names to Anastasia and Eleonora respectively.

• Jeff Randolph wrote a letter about the Dutch official who spilled hot pudding on his head. (The Dutchman did not yell that his hair was on fire.)

• Martha Randolph gave birth to the first baby born at the President's House on January 16, 1806.

• Jefferson built turning cabinets in the formal dining room. He also built many special cabinets that sprang open at his touch.

• Every year, President Jefferson had an open house on the Fourth of July and New Year's Day.

Here's a sneak preview of
Secret of the Missing Teacup

Chapter One: The Lost Coach

The coach door swung open. The little girl jumped out and ran as if she were a squirrel chased by a fox. The sash of her pink silk dress fluttered behind her as she dashed into the forest.

Next out of the coach was an older girl of ten. She was dressed as a housemaid, her long plain dress covered by a full white apron.

"Miss Adams," called the servant. "Come back here. The coach is just about to leave."

For an answer, the dark-haired Miss Adams ducked behind a bush and sat in the dirt. "I hate it in there," she cried. "We'll never get to Washington City."

The housemaid didn't try to reason with her. She took the girl by the arm and began to pull. At the first tug, the younger girl wrapped her free arm around an elm trunk and held on like a limpet to a rock.

The boy who was watching from behind the shelter of some oak trees couldn't help but laugh.

It was the servant girl who heard the noise and first noticed him.

"Look!" the girl cried, pointing. "There's a black boy hiding behind the trees."

Suddenly little Miss Adams got up and ran back to the coach quick as a jackrabbit. The maid followed, watching the boy carefully. Her eyes held curiosity but no meanness.

The boy stepped out from behind two thick trees. He didn't want anyone to think he had been spying, though he had been watching the coach circle the Maryland woods for over an hour. The coachman and his helpers, called footmen, would put the coach on a path only to make a wrong turn and become stranded in the woods again.

A woman in fine clothes slowly lowered herself out of the coach and straightened her white lace shawl. Though she was old now, the boy could tell she had once been pretty. She smiled when she saw him.

Her gentle expression gave him courage to speak. "Ma'am, are you lost?" the boy asked.

"Aye, we are," she said. "We left Baltimore and lost our way in these woods two hours ago. I think you're a servant the heavens have sent to help us. Please, will you honor us by pointing the way to Washington City?"

"Yes, ma'am," he said. "My father works there. He makes bricks for the new federal buildings." The boy was proud of his father, even though he had not seen him in over six months.

"I trust that your father is a master brick maker," she said. "I am the first lady, Abigail Adams. The president and I are to reside in the President's Palace. Will you pleasure me by telling your name?"

"Charlie, I mean Charles Anthony Brooks," he answered, lifting his chin.

"Will you guide and direct our coach driver, Charles?" Mrs. Adams asked, smiling again.

"Yes, ma'am" Charlie answered. The first lady nodded and then stepped carefully into the coach, a footman helping by guiding her elbow. The housemaid followed the first lady. Just before the girl climbed in the coach, she turned and flashed a smile. Charlie thought it was for him, but he couldn't be sure. With her pale white hair and white cap, Charlie thought she looked like a summertime daisy.

Charlie told the coach driver how to find the postal route to Washington City. The man was glad to have directions. At first he smiled and nodded his head while the boy motioned with his hands and described the turns. The coachman's smile soon turned to a frown.

"I can't remember all those directions," he said. "There are too many turns, and I'll get lost again. You must take me to the road."

"I can show you," Charlie said, "but I can't take you to Washington City. I must be home before dark."

"That is fine with me," said the driver. "I want to be well on my way before dark too."

So the young black boy pulled himself up in the seat next to the coach driver. From inside the coach came the servant girl's voice, "A boy has all the good fortune. God punishes girls by making us always stay safe and calm. Why am I never allowed to ride outside?"

"Or me?" asked four-year-old Miss Adams.

Charlie couldn't hear any more words coming from inside the coach when the horse hooves began to thud on the damp ground. The large coach with four horses moved slowly through the thick woods of elm, white oak, and maple. Charlie felt important leading the way on the hard-to-follow road. It was just two brown patches of dirt where a few wagon wheels had cut a path. He sat up straight. *What an honor,* he thought, *to be helping the first lady. God surely must watch over her and listen to her prayers.*

When they reached the road, the coachman paid Charlie a handful of coins. Then Charlie jumped down from the seat and waved good-bye to the driver. The little girl opened the coach door and pushed her head outside. "Bye-bye," she said and waved back. In her hand was a toy-sized teacup, cream-colored with a wide gold rim. Then she and the teacup disappeared into the coach, and the door closed.

The boy thought that would be the last time he would ever see the president's family and servants again. He suddenly felt sad as he headed for the shack where he lived with his mother and his three sisters. He thought about how fun it would be to live in a growing city like Washington. Nothing exciting ever happened on the small tobacco farm he worked on.

If he lived in Washington City, he might find someone to teach him a trade. In Washington City, he would get to be with his father again.

Charlie was right in the middle of a daydream about working side by side with his father when he saw something unusual lying on the dirt path. He bent down and gently picked it up. It was a white china teacup with small red flowers, just the size for tiny fingers. It had landed in a mud puddle, and Charlie saw that it had a crack and a tiny chip on the handle. *Miss Adams must have dropped this*, he thought. *I wonder if she will miss it?*

Then Charlie got an idea. *What if I take this to the President's Palace? Then I can see Father again!*

The rest of the trip home, Charlie's daydreams turned into firm plans to visit the federal city as soon as he could. He barely noticed the two men who passed him on the path riding on beautiful red horses.

They spoke in French and Charlie could only understand a few words. One of them said *President Adams*, and both men laughed. Charlie had the feeling the Frenchmen didn't like the president. He shivered as they rode away. He was glad they were going in the opposite direction. He hoped he would never meet them again.